D1188894

THE UPSIDE-DOWN MICE
And Other Animal Stories

Acknowledgements:

The author would like to thank Gina Pollinger for all her help.

Jane Merer is a journalist and writer. She lives in London with her husband and two daughters. She has been collecting stories for the Malcolm Sargent Cancer Fund for the last 20 years.

THE UPSIDE-DOWN MICE
And Other Animal Stories

Compiled by Jane Merer

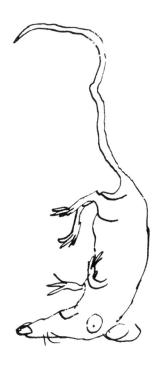

Piccadilly Press • London

CONTENTS

THE UPSIDE-DOWN MICE
by Roald Dahl

Once upon a time there lived an old man of 87 whose name was Labon. All his life he had been a quiet and peaceful person. He was very poor and very happy.

When Labon discovered that he had mice in his house, he did not at first bother himself greatly about it. But the mice multiplied. They began to bother him. They kept right on multiplying and finally there came a time when even he could stand it no longer.

'This is too much,' he said. 'This really is going a bit too far.' He hobbled out of the house down the road to a shop where he bought himself some mousetraps, a piece of cheese and some glue.

When he got home, he put the glue on the underneath of the mousetraps and stuck them to the ceiling. Then he baited them carefully with pieces of cheese and set them to go off.

That night when the mice came out of their holes and saw the mousetraps on the ceiling, they thought it a tremendous joke. They walked around on the floor, nudging each other and pointing up with their front paws and roaring with laughter. After all, it *was* pretty silly, mousetraps on the ceiling.

When Labon came down the next morning and saw that there were no mice caught in the traps, he smiled but said nothing.

He took a chair and put glue on the bottom of its legs and stuck it upside-down to the ceiling, near the mousetraps. He did the same with the table, the television set and the lamp. He took everything that was on the floor and stuck it upside-down on the ceiling. He even put a little carpet up there.

The next night when the mice came

out of their holes they were still joking and laughing about what they had seen the night before. But now, when they looked up at the ceiling, they stopped laughing very suddenly.

'Good gracious me!' cried one. 'Look up there! There's the floor!'

'Heavens above!' shouted another. 'We must be standing on the ceiling!'

'I'm beginning to feel a little giddy,' said another.

'All the blood's going to my head,' said another.

'This is terrible!' said a very senior mouse with long whiskers. 'This is really terrible! We must do something about it at once!'

'I shall faint if I have to stand on my head any longer!' shouted a young mouse.

'Me too!'

'I can't stand it!'

'Save us! Do something somebody, quick!'

They were getting hysterical now. 'I know what we'll do,' said the very

3

senior mouse. 'We'll all stand on our heads, then anyway we'll be the right way up.'

Obediently, they all stood on their heads, and after a long time, one by one, they fainted from a rush of blood to their brains.

When Labon came down the next morning the floor was littered with mice. Quickly he gathered them up and popped them all in a basket.

So the thing to remember is this: whenever the world seems to be terribly upside-down, make sure you keep your feet firmly on the ground.

ARCHIE

by Elisabeth Beresford

It had been a bad day. Short tempers in the office, a chill wind that blew in your face whichever way you turned and a shortage of buses, so that by the time Mel got home she was tired, cold and fed up. She turned into Arch Street, the wind in her face yet again and fumbled for her key and it was then that she saw it. No longer a kitten, but not yet a full grown cat. It was hunched miserably on the doorstep, its black and white fur sticking up in spikes.

'Shoo, go away ... '

The kitten cat put back its ears, but didn't move. The net curtain of the downstairs flat twitched and she caught a glimpse of old Mr Bland's cross face.

'Go on, get lost ... '

Mel opened the door and pushed her

shopping ahead of her, glancing down at the stray. It was very bedraggled, but somehow there was a certain dignity about it as it gazed up at her, its front paws neatly crossed. The wind slammed the door shut behind her and Mel began to climb the stairs, muttering under her breath.

'Dratted animal. People shouldn't have pets if they can't look after them ... '

She half-noticed that the front door of the flat opposite Mr Bland's was open and that there were packing cases on the floor. So it had been let at last ... another new tenant. They wouldn't last long. Arch Court as it was grandly named, was a restless sort of place. Only old Mr Bland never seemed to move. Mel's gloom deepened. When *he* left she would be the oldest inhabitant. She stopped on the top stair. Just because she was in a bad mood it didn't mean that she had to take it out on others ...

On the front step the kitten waited patiently. It had been waiting round most of it's young life and already it had learnt a thing or two. Like how to listen to a human voice, so it wasn't at all surprised when the front door opened slightly, quietly and it was scooped up.

'I must be out of my mind,' Mel said in the safety of her flat. 'Animals aren't allowed here, but I couldn't ... oh well. Just for tonight mind. Tomorrow you're *out*!'

She found scraps, a saucer of milk, but it wouldn't eat until it had cleaned itself meticulously, almost overbalancing as it tried to wash its back. It made Mel laugh and her gloom lessened. She told it about the in-fighting in the office and once it was on her lap, its head stretched out in bliss, it was soothing to stroke the soft coat. But she drew the line at letting it sleep on her bed and long after she had drifted off it padded round silently. Yes, this would do very well for the time being. But there needed to be a big improvement in the food.

Mel woke up rested, happier than she'd been for a long time. She opened the window and the stray stretched through the gap and along the narrow balcony, took a leap on to the shed below and vanished into the laurel bushes. It was raining now the wind had dropped.

'I can't turn you out on a day like this,' Mel said, when it returned glistening with water and shook itself on the balcony, 'but tomorrow ... !'

So it was strange that she stopped on the way back from work and bought three assorted tins of KittyCute. She was tempted by DandyCat, but really it was too expensive. She called it Archie after the flats and by the end of the week it was as if they had been together for months.

'There's definitely somebody moving in downstairs. More furniture arrived today — smart stuff too. It's probably some glamorous model. Well if it is she won't stay long!'

It was too good to last. On Saturday Mel was out all day with friends. But Archie didn't seem to mind. In fact the moment he heard the front door close he was off through the window to case the neighbourhood. He learnt to recognise her footsteps so he was always back — if a trifle breathless — when she got home. Just as if he'd never been out. On Sunday Mel washed her hair and slip-slopped round the flat talking to Archie and doing odd jobs.

'Blessed cleaner, something's got stuck in it so it blows out fluff ... '

And the doorbell rang. Mel opened the door without thinking and there was old Mr Bland, no longer cross, but triumphant. He pointed.

'I'd like to remind you that animals are not allowed. I shall have to report this to the landlord!'

Mel stood, wordless, and looked over her shoulder. Archie hadn't even had the wit to hide. He was sitting beside the cleaner on newspaper on the kitchen table. He neatly crossed his front paws and head on one side regarded Mr Bland.

'Alley cat,' said Mr Bland and stroked behind one ear. Archie looked up at him with adoration. 'Trouble with that cleaner? I could have a look at it if you like ... '

He took it to pieces, cleaned it, reassembled it, had two cups of coffee and told Mel bits of his life story. He seemed to have forgotten the landlord. He also mentioned the new, as yet unseen tenant.

'Must have a bit of cash. Nice stuff going in there ... '

Archie's ears went back. The next day he widened his territory still further. Mr Bland gave him half a tin of sardines and swore him to secrecy. Archie purred, cleaned himself meticulously and then moved quietly into the empty flat and had a good look at everything. He was so engrossed that he very nearly got caught by the new tenant. They looked at each other silently and then Archie, without losing a shred of dignity, stalked out, tail held high. The new tenant laughed and returned to the unpacking.

'And where have you been?' asked Mel, picking tiny wood shavings out of the silky fur. Archie purred for a moment or

two and then went to his plate of KittyCute again. He ate it dutifully.

'Cats used to live on scraps in my day', said old Mr Bland, who had popped in with a lamp, he had mended. He didn't add that he'd got some full cream milk in the fridge just in case Archie happened to drop by. He caught Mel's eye and they both laughed.

Downstairs the new tenant heard the sound. This place definitely had a relaxed, happy atmosphere — most unusual.

Two days later Archie went missing. To begin with Mel was quite calm. She went round calling him, then she searched the shed and the laurel bushes. She got old Mr Bland out into the cold and windy night. To hell with the landlord. They called loudly for Archie. Their voices were lost in the wind. It began to rain and the bushes danced and shimmered but there was no black and white shadow ...

'Perhaps the new tenant,' said Mel, her teeth chattering. The tenant opened the door at once and stared in amazement at the two of them. Mel with her long, dark hair in sodden ringlets, Mr Bland's hair standing up in tufts. Everybody began to talk at once.

'Wait, wait,' said the new tenant, 'you both look half frozen, the place is still a bit of a mess, but please come in. My name's

Henry by the way ... '

There might still be an open packing case or two about, but it was warm and welcoming and somehow a bottle of wine materialised.

' ... only a cat, and we're not supposed to keep pets, but he's missing ... ' Mel said as Mr Bland ran out of breath and sat down, 'he could have been run over, taken away, lost ... '

'He could also,' said Henry, refilling her glass and smiling at her in a way which made her forget she had ever been cold, 'be something of a con-cat and living in *my* kitchen for the past twenty-four hours. I've rarely seen such a pathetic stray. Fur on end, starving to death, nobody cared ... he wouldn't let me out of his sight. I'm sorry, I really did think he was homeless. Cats can be wonderful actors ... '

Right on cue Archie stalked in, tail up. He looked at them, ran a pink tongue round his mouth, sat down and delicately crossed his front paws. He began to purr at all three of them. He didn't even mind

when they began to laugh, because he'd
finally cracked it.

KittyCute upstairs for breakfast and a

chat. Sardines and full cream for lunch and, bliss, DandyCat and more talk for supper. What cat could ask for more? His purrs redoubled.

THE DISASTROUS DOG

by Penelope Lively

Some people buy dogs. Some people are
given dogs. Some people are taken over by
dogs, as you might say. I'll tell you what
happened to the Ropers, just in case *your*
parents ever decide to get a dog from the
local Animal Sanctuary.

Mr Roper was in favour of getting a
dog from the Sanctuary because he didn't
see the point of paying good money for
something when you can get it free. Mrs
Roper thought it would be nice to give a
home to a poor unwanted dog. Paul, who
was nine, didn't really care where the dog
came from so long as they had one. He'd
been wanting a dog for ages, and now that
they'd moved to a house down the end of a
long lane, with no neighbours, outside the
village, his father had come round to the

idea. A guard dog, it was to be, a sensible efficient anti-burglar useful kind of dog.

The Animal Sanctuary seethed with dogs of all shapes and sizes. They rushed around in wire netting enclosures, all barking at once, tail-wagging, jumping up and down. The Warden pointed out several promising creatures: a brown spaniel, all ears and paws, an elegant collie, a rather raffish mongrel with a penetrating bark. Mr and Mrs Roper moved along the fence, inspecting. Mrs Roper who was a pushover for both animals and children, patted and cooed and allowed herself to be licked. Paul struck up a friendship with an over-excited yellow puppy.

'Oy ...!' Paul looked around.

'Oy! You there ...'

His parents were on the far side of the yard, discussing a terrier. The Warden had gone. The voice came from none of them. And I must explain that it was, and Paul immediately understood this, no ordinary voice. It was, as it were, a voice in the head — person to person, invisible, like a telephone. But the words that were said were ordinary and straightforward. Standard English. And so was the tone, which was distinctly bossy.

He looked at the dogs, carefully. They were all dashing around except for one, a nondescript brown animal with a stumpy tail and one white ear, which stood squarely beside the fence staring at Paul.

Paul glanced over at his parents; they were not looking in his direction. He stared back at the brown dog. 'Did you say something?' he asked, feeling foolish.

'Too right I did,' said the dog. 'Do you live in a house or a flat?'

'A house. In the country.'

'Central heating? Garden?'

'Yes. Listen, how come you ...'

The dog interrupted. 'Sounds a reasonable billet. Get your parents over here and I'll do my stuff. Homeless dog act. Never fails.'

'Can they all?' asked Paul, waving at the other dogs. 'Talk?'

The dog spluttered contemptuously. 'Course not. Ordinary mob, that's all they are.'

There was something not altogether attractive about the dog's personality, but Paul could not help being intrigued. 'Then how did you learn?'

'Because I know what's what,' snapped the dog.

'And why me? Why don't you talk

to my dad?'

'Unfortunately,' said the dog, 'the adult of the species tends to have what you might call a closed mind. I've tried, believe you me. No go. It's only you small fry that are at all receptive. More's the pity. Go on — tell your mum and dad to come over and have a look at me.'

Paul wasn't entirely pleased at being called small fry. He hesitated. The dog came closer to the fence and stared up at him, with slightly narrow eyes. 'Think about it,' he said. 'We could set up in the entertainment business. There'd be something in it for you — plenty of perks. The Dog That Can Count. The Dog That Can Read Your Thoughts. We could be on the telly. The sky's the limit.'

'We just want a dog that can bark,' said Paul.

The dog flung back his head and let out a volley of ear-splitting barks. 'That do?'

Mr and Mrs Roper, abandoning the terrier, had come across. The dog

immediately hurled himself at the wire
fence with a devastating display of tail-
wagging, grinning and licking. When
Mrs Roper stooped to pat him he rolled
over on his back with his eyes shut and
squirmed in apparent ecstasy. Mrs Roper
said, 'Oh, isn't he sweet!' The dog, briefly,
opened one eye. He then got up and
squatted in front of Mr Roper in an attitude
of abject obedience. Finally, he rushed off as
though in pursuit of an unseen enemy and
did some more barking, of hideous ferocity
and quite deafening.

Well, I don't need to tell you what
happened.

To say that the dog settled in is to put
it mildly: he established himself. Within a
matter of days. He got his basket moved
from the cloakroom by feigning illness; Mrs
Roper, gazing down at him, said anxiously,
'I think perhaps he's cold in here. We'd
better let him sleep in the kitchen by the
boiler.' The dog feebly wagged his tail and
staggered to his feet. The first time they
took him for a walk he developed a limp

after the first mile. Paul examined his paws. He said, 'I can't see anything wrong.'

'Shut up,' snarled the dog. 'I'm crippled. I'm not one for all this hearty outdoor stuff, let's get that straight from the start.'

Paul had to carry him home.

On the fourth day the dog said,
'Tell her I don't like that rabbit-flavoured
meat she's giving me. I want the beef and
oxtail flavour. And more biscuits.'

'Tell her yourself,' said Paul sulkily. He
was getting tired of being ordered about.

'Some people,' snapped the dog,
'might find things going a bit awkward, if
they don't look out and act obliging. Some
people might find for instance that their
mother's best vase would get knocked off
the table and broken and *then* who'd get
the blame? Some people might find that
things mysteriously disappeared, like their
dad's pipe and people's gloves, and *then*
who'd be nagged at to get down and find
them?'

'You wouldn't!' said Paul, without
conviction.

'Try me,' said the dog.

'Why's she to believe I know what you
like and what you don't like?'

'Children have a special relationship
with animals,' said the dog. 'It's a well-

24

known fact.'

They called him Mick. It didn't seem to suit him particularly, but then it would have been hard to know what would. 'What's your name?' Paul had asked, on the first day.

'Depends,' said the dog. 'One has run through a good many, as it happens. Suit yourselves.'

So Mick it was.

His favourite activity was sleeping. Preferably after a hefty meal and on the best sofa or one of the beds. 'Most dogs,' said Paul, 'rush about all day sniffing at things and asking to be taken for walks.'

Mick yawned. 'That's their problem. Me, I've learned how to keep my head down and have a comfortable life. Push off, there's a good boy, I want a kip.'

To begin with, he barked at the postman and the milkman and the man who came to read the meter. On the fifth day, he slept through the window-cleaner and a man selling brushes and lady collecting for the Red Cross. Paul said,

'You're supposed to bark. That's what they got you for.'

'I barked my head off all yesterday,' said Mick sullenly. 'Besides, there's a rate for the job. If they want more action, then what about something extra on the side? The odd chocolate biscuit. A nice chop.'

Mr Roper, by now, was beginning to have doubts. He observed that Mick seemed a somewhat slothful sort of dog. Mrs Roper, always keen to see the best in people, wondered if perhaps he was a rather old dog and too much shouldn't be expected. Mick, looking worn, limped to his food bowl and stood there gazing at her soulfully.

Mr Roper said he was to be put out in the garden for part of every day, and no nonsense. Mick sat on the front doorstep, glowering. When visitors arrived for Sunday lunch he hurled himself at them, barking hysterically, and tore a strip out of Uncle Harry's trousers. The smallest cousin burst into tears and refused to get out of the car and Mick was shut in the garage. When he was let out he was in a towering rage. 'You're supposed to be able to tell the difference between friends and possible burglars,' said Paul. 'That was my uncle. Mum had to spend all afternoon apologising.'

'They said do guard dog stuff,' snarled

Mick, 'so I did guard dog stuff. Anyway I didn't care for the fellow.'

Other people, Paul realised, with resignation, have engaging roly-poly puppies; other people have dear old faithful sheepdogs; other people have sprightly interesting terriers. They had Mick. It was rather like having a very demanding guest in the house who is never going to leave. Only Paul, of course, knew exactly what sort of person — dog — he was, but even his parents were beginning to be a little resentful.

'He is awfully greedy,' said Mrs Roper. 'I don't know how it's happened but he's somehow got me giving him *three* meals a day now.' Paul knew only too well how it had happened.

'He's lazy,' said Mr Roper. 'No two ways about it, I'm afraid.' He took Mick for a five-mile walk; Mick rolled in a muddy ditch and then came back and rolled on the sitting-room carpet.

'That'll teach 'em,' he said. Paul, looking at his mother's face, realised with interest that Mick might go too far before long.

'I thought,' he said, 'we were going into the entertainment business. Do tricks. Go on the telly.'

Mick, sprawled on the sofa, opened one eye. 'Tricks? You must be joking, mate. That's work, that is. I know when I'm well off.'

He got fatter and fatter. His attacks on the postman were more and more unconvincing. But the crunch came on the day the men came to collect the television for repair when everyone was out. They went round to the back door, which had been left unlocked, came in, removed the television and drove away in a van. Mrs Roper, when they brought it back, apologised. 'I'm afraid our dog must have been a bit of a nuisance. I'd meant to lock him up before you came.'

The television man laughed. 'Not him. Fast asleep, he was, and then woke up and took one look and scarpered outside. Wouldn't say boo to a goose, he wouldn't.'

That did it. 'He's useless,' said Mr Roper. Mrs Roper, always prepared to give the benefit of the doubt, suggested that perhaps Mick knew the difference between television repair men and burglars. 'Not unless he could read the writing on the side of the van,' said Mr Roper grimly. 'He's going back to the Animal Sanctuary, and that's that.'

Paul, secretly, heaved a sigh of relief. Mick had gone too far. And now, with any luck, they could get another dog: a speechless dog-like dog. What would happen to Mick he could not imagine, but he had a fairly strong feeling that he was well able to take care of himself. He said to him, 'Why didn't you bite them? I mean, there they were, walking off with the telly ...'

'I wasn't going to start mixing it with blokes like that,' said Mick shortly. 'I didn't like the look in their eye. Could have done me a nasty injury. I know when to keep a low profile, I do.'

'They're going to take you back to the

Animal Sanctuary.'

Mick looked supercilious. 'No skin off my nose. To tell the truth, I've known cushier billets than this. I'll tell you what I've got my eye on for next time — nice old lady. Soft touch, old ladies can be, I've tried 'em before. Plenty of nosh and no nonsense about exercise. I'll be all right — you see.'

And something tells me that he was. But if ever you go to get a dog from an

Animal Sanctuary, and happen to run across a brown mongrel with one white ear — well, I should think very carefully ...

THE TRUE WILD LIFE
by Colin Dann

The next night Bold entered the wood with extreme caution. For, unimpressed by the gibbet, he was still realistic enough to expect the gamekeeper to react in some way to his gesture of contempt. As he crept along, not far from the badgers' home, a sharp cry of pain rent the air, followed by grunts and snorts of a most distressing kind. Bold hastened towards the sound and, along one of his regular paths, he found the sow badger caught fast in a horrible metal trap. The more she struggled, the more its vice-like grip seemed to increase. A strong, noose-like wire bore down upon her back, making her gasp for breath and almost threatening to cripple her.

Bold sniffed gingerly at the snare,

preparing to leap away on the instant if it threatened him too. The poor she-badger, panting painfully, looked at him with dull, hopeless eyes. The cub was convinced this trap had been sprung for him, and that the luckless badger had blundered into it instead. Quite unknowingly, she had saved him from almost certain death. He stood heavily in her debt. He looked more closely at the man-made device.

'I'm going to try to help you,' he told the badger coolly. 'Keep quite still.'

The trapped animal had already ceased to struggle. The pain was too severe. She heard Bold's words in amazement. What could he mean? Why didn't he run away while he was still safe? The strongest of all instincts for any wild creature on its own was self-preservation. *She* had been caught, not he. She continued to cower where she was, unable to answer him.

Bold had discovered that the strong wire that was pinning her body so cruelly to the ground was the only obstacle to her freedom. Once inside, it was impossible for the ensnared beast to free itself, for the wire could not be reached over its own back. But, from outside the trap, the wire could be sprung or snapped. Bold's only tool was the strength of his jaws.

'I'll bite this wire,' he muttered to the badger, but half to himself. He tried to get a grip on it, but it pressed too deep into her flesh and it was impossible for him to get his teeth round it without wounding her. A harsh gasp of pain escaped her lips at his first attempt. He tried again at another point. Again she winced in agony, closing her eyes. Frustrated, Bold withdrew temporarily.

He sniffed the air, while his ears constantly strained for a sound of the trap-setter. All seemed quiet. He moved forward again with increased determination. Now he noticed that at one end of the wire there was a short piece that did not pass over the sow badger's back. He fastened his side teeth on it and bit hard. Absolutely nothing happened.

'This may take a long time,' he said.

'But we have the entire night ahead of us.'

The sow badger lay fatalistically at the gamekeeper's mercy. She listened, in a quite uncomprehending manner, to the rasping of Bold's fangs on the wire. What was he doing it for, when in all probability the result would only be injury to himself as well? The night hours slowly crept by.

As Bold made one of his several pauses to rest his aching jaws, he thought he heard a steady tramp ... tramp in the distance. He froze, his every nerve and muscle quivering with tension. Yes, there was no doubt of it. Something was approaching, and that regular tread could only be the sound of human footsteps. The gamekeeper was coming to assess his handiwork!

Bold attacked the wire with renewed ferocity and desperation, knowing that at any moment he would have to flee. Then, quite suddenly, the weakened wire snapped with a fierce backward lash that nearly blinded him. Almost at the same moment, the badger pulled herself clear and, instinctively, ran straight for her set. Bold raced after her.

In the deeper darkness of the lair they lay panting side by side. Bold's eye streamed with water and, in one corner, a thin trickle of blood ran where the point of the severed wire had pierced. The badger's back, too, had been cut and throbbed insistently.

'Why? Why?' she kept muttering.

Bold did not answer, but rubbed his bad eye with the back of one paw as if it would heal it.

Overcome by their experiences, they fell into an uneasy sleep.

The sow badger awoke first. Her back still smarted, but the realisation that she was still alive flooded over her joyously. It was as though she had cheated death. But — no! *She* hadn't cheated it. She remembered her companion. She smelt the blood on his face and began to lick at his fur, gently and with gratitude. Bold awoke and shook his head in an attempt to free himself of the pain.

'Why did you do it?' she asked him.

He looked at her for a moment. 'That trap was laid for me,' he replied.

The badger still couldn't fathom his meaning. 'Surely, then,' she faltered, 'that was your escape?'

'Yes,' he said. 'I escaped death — because of you.'

'Then why should I live?' she persisted in bewilderment.

Now it was Bold's turn to have no understanding. 'But why should you die,' he emphasised, 'because of my good fortune?'

'That's Life,' she answered in a matter-of-fact way.

'No. That's Death,' he corrected her. 'And too great a sacrifice.'

'My carelessness led me into the trap,' said the badger. 'I had only myself to blame.'

'I owed it to you to help *you* to escape as long as I ran free,' Bold tried to explain. But he could see that she still didn't understand. Was this, then, the True Wild

Life after all? This natural indifference to
another's suffering, even to another's fate,
when the cause of it had been oneself? In
his upbringing, the law instilled by his
father and enshrined in the oath, had been
to help one's friends in trouble, and to
expect the same from them. But even there,

in the Nature Reserve, he seemed to remember that the law only applied to a particular group of creatures — those animals and birds who had banded together long ago to travel across country to the safety of the Park.

The badger interrupted his thoughts. 'I shall be forever grateful to you,' she was saying, 'and I'm now very much in your debt.' She paused. 'If I follow your example — and it seems I must — I offer you my help, and that of my clan, if ever you need it.'

'I am glad I freed you,' said Bold simply. 'And I — '

'And you've wounded yourself in doing so, I fear to say,' she broke in.

'It will heal,' he said.

'Does my licking help?' she asked him.

'It does soothe,' he answered.

She resumed her task.

'Tomorrow I move on,' the cub said decisively. 'This episode has taught me I shouldn't linger here.'

'You are wise,' she answered.

'But first,' said Bold with bravado, 'I shall have one more meal of pheasant.'

'And I,' responded the badger, 'shall help you catch it.'

THE JENIUS

by Dick King-Smith

That night, before she went to bed, Judy wrote the great news in her diary. She was very faithful about putting something in it every day, even if sometimes it was only a bit about the weather. But that Joe and Molly should have had a baby — that was great news and deserved a lot of space.

JUDY'S DAIRY. PRIVIT.

JUNE 10th: Great surprise! Molly had a baby! Found him first thing this morning and I am going to train him. Already he sits when he is told. He is briliant. He is mostly white like Molly but he has a sort of main like a horse running all down his back and that is redish like Joe.

I asked Dad what you call some one who is really briliant and he said 'A jenius'. Why? and I said 'because that is what I'm going to call my new baby guinea-pig' and he laughed but I said 'You just wait. One day the World will know June 10th is the birthday of Jenius.'

June 10th was in fact a very good time for Jenius to have been born, because it meant that he was around six weeks old by the time the long summer holidays began.

Now his trainer would be able to concentrate on him without the interruption of school.

During these six weeks Jenius had grown amazingly. All baby guinea-pigs do, of course, but he had benefited particularly, first from being an only child and so getting all his mother's milk, and secondly from Judy's spoiling.

Ordinary guinea-pigs, for example, might get the occasional piece of stale bread. Jenius got regular digestive biscuits. These were his rewards after the daily 'training' sessions.

Jenius at last mastered the most difficult trick of the exercises that Judy set him. This was the ending to the trick called 'Trust'.

Not only had he to balance a piece of biscuit on the end of his nose, but then, when Judy said 'Paid for!', he had to toss up the food with a jerk of his head and catch it in his mouth. Jenius never tired of telling his mother and father how easy this trick was.

'Mind you,' he said, 'I'm the only guinea-pig in the world who can do it, I'm sure of that.'

'Very nice, dear,' said Molly absently.

'Pride,' muttered Joe darkly, 'comes before a fall.'

SEPTEMBER 3rd:
Tomorrow is the last day of the Hollidays and I am going to give him a Test. I am going the to make him do all the things he has been taut and he has got to do them correcktly and I shall give him marks for his performants in each one.

SEPTEMBER 4th: Jenius lived up to his name! He performed perfictly and got Full Marks and I am going to ask my teacher if I can take him to school and show them how briliant he is and how briliantly I have trained him. I'm the only person in the World who could have done it, I'm sure of that.

Jenius, it must be said, was not the only one who had become a bit of a bighead, and by the end of the first day back at school everyone in the class was fed up with hearing how clever both he and Judy were. Before long Judy's teacher too had had enough.

'Judy,' she said. 'You don't really expect us to believe all this, do you?'

'Yes,' said Judy. 'It's true.'

'Well, I'll tell you what. You bring this amazing animal of yours into school and then you can show us all these tricks that you say he can do.'

At once everyone wanted to get in on the act and bring their pet to school.

'Oh, can I bring my rabbit?'
' ... my gerbil?'
' ... my hamster?'
' ... my budgie?'
Until the teacher said 'All right. We'll have a Pets' Day. You can each bring a pet in to school, provided you bring it in a cage or a box — we don't want anything too big, mind, no Shetland Ponies or Great Danes. Who knows, Judy, someone else may have a clever animal too.'

Judy laughed. 'Not as clever as Jenius,' she said scornfully. 'Not possibly. You just wait and see.'

Like most people who keep diaries, Judy usually wrote in hers each evening. But as soon as she woke on the morning that had been chosen for Pets' Day, she opened it.

SEPTEMBER 11 th: Today it is Pets' Day at school! Jenius will tryumph! * Watch this space! *

At breakfast time she could not contain herself. Till now she had said nothing to her parents — as she had sworn on July 23rd — of the progress of the Jenius, but she just knew she would not be able to resist describing the success that was to come before another hour had passed.

'What d'you think is happening today?' she said.

'You're going to be late for school,' said her mother, 'if you don't hurry up. And clean your shoes before you go. And take your anorak — it looks like rain.'

'I'm taking Jenius to school,' said Judy.

'Very nice, dear,' said her mother. 'Now, do you want an apple or a banana in your lunch box?'

'Apple,' said Judy. 'Dad, did you hear what I said?'

'I did,' said her father from behind his morning paper. 'Will he have to start in the Infants or is he clever enough to go straight into your class?'

'Oh Dad!' cried Judy. 'Honestly, I really

have trained him,' and she rattled off a list
of the things that Jenius could do.

'Judy,' said her father. 'You don't
really expect us to believe all this, do you?'

'Yes,' said Judy. 'It's true.' Her father
folded his newspaper.

'Now look here,' he said. 'Playing
pretend games with your precious pet
is one thing. But you mustn't confuse
fantasy with truth.'

There was hardly room to move in Judy's classroom that morning. Everywhere there were hutches and cages and baskets and boxes containing pets. Only the Jenius was free, sitting perfectly still in front of Judy.

Judy's teacher saw what seemed to her a rather odd-looking whitish guinea-pig, with a crest of reddish hair sticking up along its back, and said 'Is this the genius we've heard such a lot about?'

'Yes,' said Judy proudly. 'Shall I show you what he can do?'

'All right,' said her teacher. 'Put him on that big table in the middle of the room where everyone can see him.'

Ranged around the edges of the big table were several pet-containers, a couple of hamster-cages, a glass jar that held stick insects, and a square basket that had one open side barred with metal rods.

Fate decreed that Judy should put Jenius down quite near to this basket and facing it, and though no one else could see what was in it, he could. He looked

through the bars and saw a face, a
merciless face, with glowing yellow eyes
and a wide mouth filled with sharp white
teeth.

In fact the occupant of the basket was
only a half-grown kitten, but the sight of it
turned Jenius's legs to jelly and scrambled
his brains. He was so frightened that he
promptly Died For His Country, and there
he lay, quite still and barely breathing. He
could hear Judy's voice saying 'Come!' and

then, more loudly, 'Jenius! Come!!' Then he heard a rising tide of noise which was the whole class first sniggering, then giggling, and finally laughing their heads off at clever Judy and her clever guinea-pig, about which she had boasted so loud and long. But he could not move a muscle.

'The great animal trainer!' someone said, and they laughed even more.

'Perhaps that will teach you a lesson, Judy,' said the teacher at last. 'He doesn't seem to be quite the genius you told us he was. You mustn't confuse fantasy with truth.'

'How did you get on, dear, your first day at school?' said Molly that evening.

'Need you ask?' growled Joe. 'You were top of the class, weren't you, son? Got full marks for everything? Performed perfectly, eh?'

'No,' said the Jenius in a small choked voice. 'I didn't do anything.'

'Well well well,' said Joe. 'The only guinea-pig in the world who can do all

those tricks and he didn't do anything.
I quite expected you to tell us you did
something fantastic ... Hopping like a
rabbit perhaps. Or flying like a bird, I
shouldn't be surprised.'

Judy came in at that moment with a
bunch of dandelions, to hear Joe and Molly
making an awful racket. She thought they
were yelling for food as usual but actually
they were in fits of laughter.

'Flying! Oh Joe, you are a scream!'
squealed Molly, and Joe, snorting with
mirth, chuckled 'Pride comes before a
crash-landing!'

A few minutes later Judy's father,
home from work, put his head in at the
door of the shed.

'Well?' he said. 'And did our genius
perform all his amazing tricks?'

'No,' said Judy. 'He wouldn't do
anything.'

'Perhaps that will teach you a lesson,
Judy,' said her father.

Judy took a deep breath.

'Perhaps it has, Dad,' she said. 'But

I wouldn't like you to think I was a liar.'

'It's difficult for me not to think that,' said her father, 'when you tell me such fantastic things. For instance, that your guinea-pig can balance something on his nose and then throw it up and catch it. If he can do that, I'll eat my hat, I promise you.'

'Watch,' said Judy. She took a digestive out of her pocket and broke a piece off. She opened the door of Jenius's hutch.

'Come!' she said, and he came.

'Sit!' she said, and he sat.

Carefully she placed the fragment of biscuit on top of Jenius's snout.

'Trust!' she said, and he remained sitting bolt upright and stock-still for perhaps ten seconds, till Judy cried 'Paid for!'

Up in the air sailed the bit of digestive and down it came again, straight into the open mouth of Jenius.

'*What* a good boy!' said Judy. 'Now you can eat it up.'

She turned to her father, who was bending down, hands on knees, watching

in open-mouthed amazement, hat in hand.
She took it from him.

'And you,' she said, 'can eat that.'

THE LAST OF THE DRAGONS
by E. Nesbit

Of course you know that dragons were once as common as motor-omnibuses are now, and almost as dangerous. But as every well-brought-up prince was expected to kill a dragon, and rescue a princess, the dragons grew fewer and fewer till it was often quite hard for a princess to find a dragon to be rescued from. And at last there were no more dragons in France and no more dragons in Germany, or Spain, or Italy, or Russia. There were some left in China, and are still, but they are cold and bronzy, and there were never any, of course, in America. But the last real live dragon left was in England, and of course that was a very long time ago, before what you call English History began. This dragon lived

in Cornwall in the big caves amidst the rocks, and a very fine dragon it was, quite seventy feet long from the tip of its fearful snout to the end of its terrible tail. It breathed fire and smoke, and rattled when it walked, because its scales were made of iron. Its wings were like half-umbrellas — or like bats' wings, only several thousand times bigger. Everyone was very frightened of it, and well they might be.

Now the King of Cornwall had one daughter, and when she was sixteen, of course she would have to go and face the dragon: such tales are always told in royal nurseries at twilight, so the Princess knew what she had to expect. The dragon would not eat her, of course — because the prince would come and rescue her. But the Princess could not help thinking it would be much pleasanter to have nothing to do with the dragon at all — not even to be rescued from him. 'All the princes I know are such very silly little boys,' she told her father. 'Why must I be rescued by a prince?'

'It's always done, my dear,' said the King, taking his crown off and putting it on the grass, for they were alone in the garden, and even kings must unbend sometimes.

'Father, darling,' said the Princess presently, when she had made a daisy chain and put it on the King's head, where the crown ought to have been. 'Father, darling, couldn't we tie up one of the silly little princes for the dragon to look at — and then I could go and kill the dragon and rescue the prince? I fence much better than any of the princes we know.'

'What an unladylike idea!' said the King, and put his crown on again, for he saw the Prime Minister coming with a basket of new-laid Bills for him to sign. 'Dismiss the thought, my child. I rescued your mother from a dragon, and you don't want to set yourself up above her, I should hope?'

'But this is the *last* dragon. It is different from all other dragons.'

'How?' asked the King.

'Because he *is* the last,' said the Princess, and went off to her fencing lessons, with which she took great pains. She took great pains with all her lessons —

for she could not give up the idea of fighting the dragon. She took such pains that she became the strongest and boldest and most skilful and most sensible princess in Europe. She had always been the prettiest and nicest.

And the days and years went on, till at last the day came which was the day before the Princess was to be rescued from the dragon. The Prince who was to do this deed of valour was a pale prince, with large eyes and a head full of mathematics and philosophy, but he had unfortunately neglected his fencing lessons. He was to stay the night at the palace, and there was a banquet.

After supper the Princess sent her pet parrot to the Prince with a note. It said:

Please, Prince, come on to the terrace. I want to talk to you without anybody else hearing. — The Princess.

So, of course, he went — and he saw her gown of silver a long way off shining among the shadows of the trees like water in starlight. And when he came quite close to her he said: 'Princess, at your service,' and bent his cloth-of-gold-covered knee and put his hand on his cloth-of-gold-covered heart.

'Do you think,' said the Princess earnestly, 'that you will be able to kill the dragon?'

'I will kill the dragon,' said the Prince firmly, 'or perish in the attempt.'

'It's no use your perishing,' said the Princess.

'It's the least I can do,' said the Prince.

'What I'm afraid of is that it'll be the most you can do,' said the Princess.

'It's the only thing I can do,' said he, 'unless I kill the dragon.'

'Why you should do anything for me is what I can't see,' said she.

'But I want to,' he said. 'You must know that I love you better than anything in the world.'

When he said that he looked so kind that the Princess began to like him a little.

'Look here,' she said, 'no one else will go out tomorrow. You know they tie me to a rock and leave me — and then everybody scurries home and puts up the shutters and keeps them shut till you ride through the town in triumph shouting that you've killed the dragon, and I ride on the horse behind you weeping for joy.'

'I've heard that that is how it is done,' said he.

'Well, do you love me well enough to come very quickly and set me free — and we'll fight the dragon together?'

'It wouldn't be safe for you.'

'Much safer for both of us for me to be free, with a sword in my hand, than tied up and helpless. *Do* agree.'

He could refuse her nothing. So he agreed. And next day everything happened as she had said.

When he had cut the cords that tied her to the rock they stood on the lonely mountain-side looking at each other.

'It seems to me,' said the Prince, 'that this ceremony could have been arranged without the dragon.'

'Yes,' said the Princess, 'but since it has been arranged with the dragon — '

'It seems such a pity to kill the dragon — the last in the world,' said the Prince.

'Well then, don't let's,' said the Princess; 'let's tame it not to eat princesses but to eat out of their hands. They say everything can be tamed by kindness.'

'Taming by kindness means giving them things to eat,' said the Prince. 'Have you got anything to eat?'

She hadn't, but the Prince owned that he had a few biscuits. 'Breakfast was so very early,' said he, 'and I thought you might have felt faint after the fight.'

'How clever,' said the Princess, and they took a biscuit in each hand. And they looked here, and they looked there, but never a dragon could they see.

'But here's its trail,' said the Prince, and pointed to where the rock was scarred and scratched so as to make a track leading to a dark cave. It was like cart-ruts in a Sussex road, mixed with the marks of sea-gull's feet on the sea-sand. 'Look, that's where it's dragged its brass tail and planted its steel claws.'

'Don't let's think how hard its tail and its claws are,' said the Princess, 'or I shall begin to be frightened — and I know you can't tame anything, even by kindness, if you're frightened of it. Come on. Now or never.'

She caught the Prince's hand in hers and they ran along the path towards the dark mouth of the cave. But they did not run into it. It really was so very *dark*.

So they stood outside, and the Prince shouted: 'What ho! Dragon there! What ho within!' And from the cave they heard an answering voice and great clattering and creaking. It sounded as though a rather large cotton-mill were stretching itself and waking up out of its sleep.

The Prince and the Princess trembled, but they stood firm.

'Dragon — I say, dragon!' said the Princess, 'do come out and talk to us. We've brought you a present.'

'Oh yes — I know your presents,' growled the dragon in a huge rumbling voice. 'One of those precious princesses, I suppose? And I've got to come out and fight for her. Well, I tell you straight, I'm not going to do it. A fair fight I wouldn't say no to — a fair fight and no favour — but one of these put-up fights where you've got to lose — no! So I tell you. If I wanted a princess I'd come and take her, in my own time — but I don't. What do you suppose I'd do with her, if I'd got her?'

'Eat her, wouldn't you?' said the Princess, in a voice that trembled a little.

'Eat a fiddle-stick end,' said the dragon very rudely. 'I wouldn't touch the horrid thing.'

The Princess's voice grew firmer.

'Do you like biscuits?' she said.

'No,' growled the dragon.

'Not the nice little expensive ones with sugar on the top?'

'*No,*' growled the dragon.

'Then what *do* you like?' asked the Prince.

'You go away and don't bother me,' growled the dragon, and they could hear it turn over, and the clang and clatter of its turning echoed in the cave like the sound of the steam-hammers in the Arsenal at Woolwich.

The Prince and Princess looked at each other. What *were* they to do? Of course it was no use going home and telling the King that the dragon didn't want princesses — because His Majesty was very old-fashioned and would never have believed that a new-fashioned dragon could ever be at all different from an old-fashioned dragon. They could not go into the cave and kill the dragon. Indeed, unless he attacked the Princess it did not seem fair to kill him at all.

'He must like something,' whispered the Princess, and she called out in a voice as sweet as honey and sugar-cane:

'Dragon! Dragon dear!'

'WHAT?' shouted the dragon. 'Say that again!' and they could hear the dragon coming towards them through the darkness of the cave. The Princess shivered, and said in a very small voice:

'Dragon — Dragon dear!'

And then the dragon came out. The Prince drew his sword, and the Princess drew hers — the beautiful silver-handled one that the Prince had brought in his motor-car. But they did not attack; they moved slowly back as the dragon came out, all the vast scaly length of him, and lay along the rock — his great wings halfspread and his silvery sheen gleaming like diamonds in the sun. At last they could retreat no further — the dark rock behind them stopped their way — and with their backs to the rock they stood swords in hand and waited.

The dragon drew nearer and nearer — and now they could see that he was not breathing fire and smoke as they had expected — he came crawling slowly towards them wriggling a little as a puppy does when it wants to play and isn't quite sure whether you're not cross with it.

And then they saw that great tears

were coursing down its brazen cheek.

'Whatever's the matter?' said the Prince.

'Nobody,' sobbed the dragon, 'ever called me "dear" before!'

'Don't cry, dragon dear,' said the Princess. 'We'll call you "dear" as often as you like. We want to tame you.'

'I *am* tame,' said the dragon —'that's just it. That's what nobody but you has ever found out. I'm so tame that I'd eat out of your hands.'

'Eat what, dragon dear?' said the Princess. 'Not biscuits?' The dragon slowly shook his heavy head.

'Not biscuits?' said the Princess tenderly. 'What, then, dragon dear?'

'Your kindness quite undragons me,' it said. 'No one has ever asked any of us what we like to eat — always offering us princesses, and then rescuing them — and never once, "What'll you take to drink the King's health in?" Cruel hard, I call it,' and it wept again.

'But what would you like to drink our

health in?' said the Prince. 'We're going to be married today, aren't we, Princess?'

She said that she supposed so.

'What'll I take to drink your health in?' asked the dragon. 'Ah, you're something like a gentleman, you are, sir. I don't mind if I do, sir. I'll be proud to drink your and your good lady's health in a tiny drop of' — its voice faltered — 'to think of you asking me so friendly like,' it said. 'Yes, sir, just a tiny drop of puppuppuppuppupetrol – tha-that's what does a dragon good, sir — '

'I've lots in the car,' said the Prince, and was off down the mountain like a flash. He was a good judge of character and knew that with this dragon the Princess would be safe.

'If I might make so bold,' said the dragon, 'while the gentleman's away — p'raps just to pass the time you'd be so kind as to call me Dear again, and if you'd shake claws with a poor old dragon that's never been anybody's enemy but his own — well, the last of the dragons'll be the proudest dragon that's ever been since the first of them.'

It held out an enormous paw, and the great steel hooks that were its claws closed over the Princess's hand as softly as the claws of the Himalayan bear will close over the bit of bun you hand it through the bars at the Zoo.

And so the Prince and Princess went back to the palace in triumph, the dragon following them like a pet dog. And all through the wedding festivities no one drank more earnestly to the happiness of the bride and bridegroom than the Princess's pet dragon — whom she had at once named Fido.

And when the happy pair were settled in their own kingdom, Fido came to them and begged to be allowed to make himself useful.

'There must be some little thing I can do,' he said, rattling his wings and stretching his claws. 'My wings and claws and so on ought to be turned to some account —

to say nothing of my grateful heart.'

So the Prince had a special saddle or
howdah made for him — very long it was
— like the tops of many tramcars fitted
together. One hundred and fifty seats were
fitted to this, and the dragon, whose great-
est pleasure was now to give pleasure to
others, delighted in taking parties of children to the seaside. It flew through the air
quite easily with its hundred and fifty little
passengers — and would lie on the sand
patiently waiting till they were ready to
return. The children were very fond of it,
and used to call it Dear, a word which
never failed to bring tears of affection and
gratitude to its eyes. So it lived, useful
and respected, till quite the other day —
when someone happened to say, in his
hearing, that dragons were out-of-date,
now so much new machinery had come in.
This so distressed him that he asked
the King to change him into something less
old-fashioned, and the kindly monarch at
once changed him into a mechanical

contrivance. The dragon, indeed, became the first aeroplane.

DESPERATE FOR A DOG

by Rose Impey

Me and my sister were desperate for a
dog, but Mum and Dad wouldn't let us
have one. Until we set out to persuade
them ...

At bedtime my sister and I took the
paper upstairs with us. Instead of a
bedtime story I read her the adverts.

'Last of the litter sheltie puppy (bitch) —
must find home soon. Looking for someone
to love her.
Tel. 696487
6-10p.m.'

When I'd finished she said, 'Read me
the one about the sheltie puppy again.'
Then she said to me, 'Let's ring it.'

'What do you mean?' I said.

'Let's ring the number — 696487 — on the phone.'

So we did.

We crept along the landing and used the phone in Mum's new study. We talked very quietly so Mum and Dad wouldn't hear. The lady on the phone told us all about the puppy. It sounded so cute.

'Ahhhhhhh,' I said.

'Ohhhhhhh,' said my sister.

We talked to her for ages. Then we crept back to bed.

The next day we were just sitting down for lunch when the doorbell rang.

Mum went to the door.

Then she called Dad.

It was the lady from the paper.

She'd brought the puppy with her. Mum looked red. She didn't know what to say.

Dad looked red. He had plenty to say. 'It was very naughty of you to waste that lady's time. I've told you before, we are not having a dog. Certainly not. No chance. When I say no — I mean no. And I will not change my mind. Now do you understand?'

My sister burst out crying again.

That was round one to Dad.

Next Round

Not long after that a wonderful thing happened. Well, it was wonderful for me and my sister. It wasn't very nice for Mrs Roper, the lady who lives next door.

She had to go into hospital to have an operation. Me and my sister made get well cards and sent them with Mum when she visited.

The wonderful part of it was that we had to look after her dog!

Toby was a big black Labrador.

He was quite old, in dog years.

He'd never been in kennels.

Mrs Roper refused to go into hospital until Mum promised that we'd look after Toby.

Dad wasn't very pleased.

'Dogs,' he said. 'I'm sick of hearing about dogs. Still, I suppose it will make some people happy.'

HAPPY! We were over the Moon. We couldn't stop laughing when Mum told us.

79

'It's okay for you but I'm the one at home all day. I'll have to look after the old fleabag.'

'Oh, Dad!' we said.

Even Mum was shocked.

'It was a joke,' said Dad.

Me and my sister would have been happy to stay at home all day with Toby.

In fact each morning my sister said she had a tummy ache or a cold coming or a sore ankle.

Dad wasn't fooled once.

Every day he made her go to school. But each night when we got home we washed Toby's bowls and mixed his food and brushed his coat and took him for walks.

When he was in a good mood Toby would chase a stick or a ball, if it didn't go too far.

He never brought it back.

Toby didn't really like exercise.

Mostly Toby liked to sleep.

Sometimes he slept in his basket in the kitchen.

Sometimes he slept in front of the gas fire.

And sometimes he slept right against the fence, as close as he could get to his own home.

When we were at school, Toby liked to sleep in Dad's shed.

'He's always there under my feet,' Dad complained.

At teatime each day Dad told us stories about what Toby had done that day: how he'd chewed the handle off Dad's best screwdriver, or dug holes in the flower-bed to bury bits of Dad's wood, or eaten a whole tin of wax polish and then been sick in the sandpit.

We thought they were funny stories. But Dad didn't.

'That dog would eat anything,' said Dad. 'He must be the thickest dog in the world. I don't think he's got anything between his ears except sawdust.'

After Toby had been with us for three weeks he felt like one of the family.

Mum saved all the scraps for him. She made a real fuss of him.

Even Dad stopped moaning.

He didn't exactly seem to like Toby, he just put up with him.

But Toby certainly liked Dad. He followed him everywhere. When Dad sat down in the evening Toby shuffled up and lay down on Dad's feet like a black velvet foot-warmer.

One day me and my sister ran all the way home from school. To see how fast we could do it.

We raced into the house to surprise Dad.

We could hardly believe our eyes.

Dad and Toby were rolling on the floor playing a silly game.

Dad was laughing his head off and pushing Toby in a really friendly way.

Toby was trying to bite Dad's ear.
'Get off, you soft old thing.'

When Dad saw us he went red. He looked so embarrassed ... seeing us ... seeing him ... fooling about with Toby.

'I thought you said Toby was an old fleabag with no brains.'

'I thought you said you didn't like dogs.'

'You're a fibber!'

Dad said nothing.

What could he say?

We'd caught him out.

He couldn't fool us any more.

Me and my sister stood there grinning.

We won that round.

AT THE ZOO

by Brian Patten

Two new creatures had arrived at the zoo, and Class 10XA were clustered around the cage, studying them.

'Don't go so near the cage,' said the teacher.

'They don't look dangerous,' said one of the pupils.

'They look sweet,' said another.

'They might look sweet,' said the teacher, 'but that's because they are young, and even the young ones are known to be quite vicious at times. They are carnivorous from a very early age, remember.'

'What's carnivorous?' asked one of the pupils.

'It means they eat meat.'

'Does that mean they would eat us?'

'Quite possibly,' said the teacher.

'They look tame,' said another pupil.
'They've hardly moved since we came.'
    'That's because they are more
interested in the box in the corner of their

cage than in us, I suspect, said the teacher.

'If you put one of those boxes in front of them, they will sit still for hours. It's when you take the box away that they go a bit wild.'

'Well, I think they are very sweet,' said one of the class. 'They look slightly like the monkeys in the other cage. Are they as intelligent?'

'Oh, no,' said the teacher. 'They can't do half the things the monkeys can.'

'I think they are quite boring myself,' said another of the pupils, 'and all that pink skin — yuk! They're so ugly!'

'Maybe they'd be more interesting if they weren't gaping at that box,' said the teacher. 'But they do move about, usually in the daylight. Anyway, they are part of our zoo project, and you must all use your computer note-pads to describe them.'

Class 10XA soon got bored looking at the new arrivals and moved along to another cage.

As they drifted away, one of the

pupils asked, 'Where did you say they came from?'

'I've already told you,' said the teacher. 'Honestly, Harsog! Sometimes I think you've no brains in any of your three heads! They are from a planet called Earth, and they are called children. Now, don't let me have to tell you again!'

LION AT SCHOOL

by Philippa Pearce

Once upon a time there was a little girl
who didn't like going to school. She always
set off late. Then she had to hurry, but she
never hurried fast enough.

One morning she was hurrying along as
usual when she turned a corner and there
stood a lion, blocking her way. He stood
waiting for her. He stared at her with his
yellow eyes. He growled, and when he
growled the little girl could see that his
teeth were as sharp as skewers and knives.
He growled: 'I'm going to eat you up.'

    'Oh dear!' said the little girl, and she
began to cry.

    'Wait!' said the lion. 'I haven't finished.
I'm going to eat you up UNLESS you take
me to school with you.'

'Oh dear!' said the little girl. 'I couldn't do that. My teacher says we mustn't bring pets to school.'

'I'm not a pet,' said the lion. He growled again, and she saw that his tail swished from side to side in anger — *swish*! *swash*! 'You can tell your teacher that I'm a friend who is coming to school with you,' he said. 'Now shall we go?'

The little girl had stopped crying. She said: 'All right. But you must promise two things. First of all, you mustn't eat anyone: it's not allowed.'

'I suppose I can growl?' said the lion.

'I suppose you can,' said the little girl.

'And I suppose I can roar?'

'Must you?' said the little girl.

'Yes,' said the lion.

'Then I suppose you can,' said the little girl.

'And what's the second thing?' asked the lion.

'You must let me ride on your back to school.'

'Very well,' said the lion.

He crouched down on the pavement
and the little girl climbed on to his back.
She held on by his mane. Then they went
on together towards the school, the little
girl riding the lion.

The lion ran with the little girl on his back to school. Even so, they were late. The little girl and the lion went into the classroom just as the teacher was calling the register.

The teacher stopped calling the register when she saw the little girl and the lion. She stared at the lion, and all the other

children stared at the lion, wondering what the teacher was going to say. The teacher said to the little girl: 'You know you are not allowed to bring pets to school.'

The lion began to swish his tail — *swish*! *swash*! The little girl said: 'This is not a pet. This is my friend who is coming to school with me.'

The teacher still stared at the lion, but she said to the little girl: 'What is his name, then?'

'Noil,' said the little girl. 'His name is Noil. Just Noil.' She knew it would be no good to tell the teacher that her friend was a lion, so she had turned his name backwards: LION — NOIL.

The teacher wrote the name down in the register: NOIL. Then she finished calling the register.

'Betty Small,' she said.

'Yes,' said the little girl.

'Noil,' said the teacher.

'Yes,' said the lion. He mumbled, opening his mouth as little as possible, so that the teacher should not see his teeth as sharp as skewers and knives.

All that morning the lion sat up on
his chair next to the little girl, like a big cat,
with his tail curled round his paws,

as good as gold. He didn't speak unless the teacher spoke to him. He didn't growl, he didn't roar.

At playtime the little girl and the lion went into the playground. All the children stopped playing to stare at the lion. Then they went on playing again. The little girl stood in a corner of the playground, with the lion beside her.

'Why don't we play like the others?' the lion asked.

The little girl said, 'I don't like playing because some of the big boys are so big and rough. They knock you over without meaning to.'

The lion growled. 'They wouldn't knock ME over,' he said.

'There's one big boy — the very biggest,' said the little girl. 'His name is Jack Tall. He knocks me over on purpose.'

'Which is he?' said the lion. 'Point him out to me.'

The little girl pointed out Jack Tall to the lion.

'Ah!' said the lion. 'So that's Jack Tall.'

Just then the bell rang again, and all the children went back to their classrooms. The lion went with the little girl and sat beside her.

Then the children drew and wrote until dinner-time. The lion was hungry, so he wanted to draw a picture of his dinner.

'What will it be for dinner?' he asked the little girl. 'I hope it's meat.'

'No said the little girl. 'It will be fish fingers because today is Friday.'

Then the little girl showed the lion how to hold the yellow crayon in his paw and draw fish fingers. Underneath his picture she wrote: 'I like meat better than fish fingers.'

Then it was dinner-time. The lion sat up on his chair at the dinner-table next to the little girl.

The lion ate very fast and at the end he said: 'I'm still hungry; and I wish it had been meat.'

After dinner all the children went into the playground.

All the big boys were running about, and the very biggest boy, Jack Tall, came running towards the little girl. He was running in circles, closer to the little girl.

'Go away,' said the lion. 'You might knock my friend over. Go away.'

'Shan't,' said Jack Tall. The little

girl got behind the lion.

Jack Tall was running closer and closer and closer.

The lion growled. Then Jack Tall saw the lion's teeth as sharp as skewers and knives. He stopped running. He stood still. He stared.

The lion opened his mouth wider — so wide that Jack Tall could see his throat, opened wide and deep and dark like a tunnel to go into. Jack Tall went pale.

Then the lion roared.

He roared and he ROARED and he *ROARED.*

All the teachers came running out.

All the children stopped playing and stuck their fingers in their ears. And the biggest boy, Jack Tall, turned round and ran and ran and ran. He never stopped running until he got home to his mother.

The little girl came out from behind the lion.

'Well,' she said, 'I don't think much of *him*. I shall never be scared of *him* again.'

'I was hungry,' said the lion, 'I could

easily have eaten him. Only I'd promised you.'

'And his mother wouldn't have liked it,' said the little girl. 'Time for afternoon school now.'

'I'm not staying for afternoon school,'

said the lion.

'See you on Monday then,' said the little girl. But the lion did not answer. He just walked off.

On Monday the lion did not come to school. At playtime, in the playground, the biggest boy came up to the little girl.

'Where's your friend that talks so loudly?' he said.

'He's not here today,' said the little girl.

'Might he come another day?' asked the biggest boy.

'He might,' said the little girl. 'He easily might. So you just watch out, Jack Tall.'